Code It!
Create It!

Ideas + Inspiration
for Coding

by Sarah Hutt

illustrated by Brenna Vaughan

Penguin Workshop
An Imprint of Penguin Random House

PENGUIN WORKSHOP
Penguin Young Readers Group
An Imprint of Penguin Random House LLC

Copyright © 2017 by Penguin Random House LLC and Girls Who Code Inc.
All rights reserved. Published by Penguin Workshop, an imprint of Penguin Random House LLC, 345 Hudson Street, New York, New York 10014. PENGUIN and PENGUIN WORKSHOP are trademarks of Penguin Books Ltd, and the W colophon is a trademark of Penguin Random House LLC. Manufactured in China.

ISBN 9780399542558   10 9 8 7 6 5 4 3 2 1

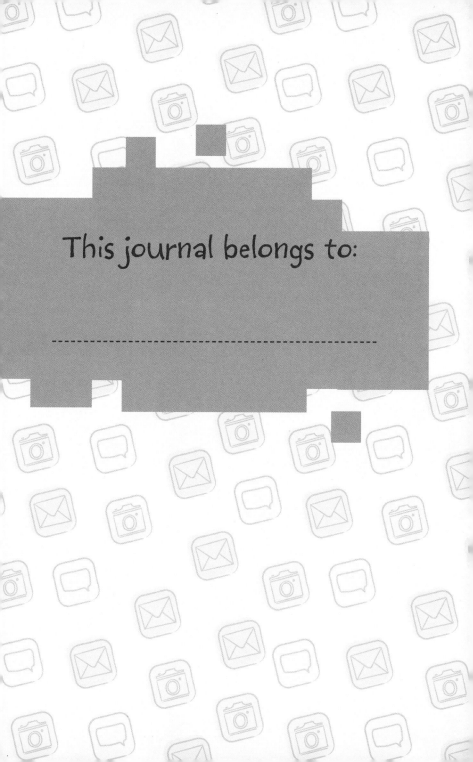

This journal belongs to:

Hi, I'm Reshma. I'm the founder of Girls Who Code.

Do you think coding is a way to be creative? It's okay if you don't. In our clubs at Girls Who Code, we teach middle- and high-school girls how to tap into their creativity by writing code and creating digital games, apps, websites, and more. But when most girls start in our programs, they think coding is boring and means being alone in a basement for hours in front of a computer. That couldn't be further from the truth!

Like the girls in our programs, you'll quickly learn that coding is all about creativity. It's a way to make the ideas in your head come to life! For example, do you like animals? Then you can make a website to help dogs at shelters find homes. Do you care about environmental issues? Create an app for people to keep track of their environmental impact. Or maybe you're into fashion? Make clothing that adjusts to people's temperature, or even that lights up when you dance. Whatever you can imagine, you can code!

Whether you don't know how to get started with coding or already have a ton of ideas, this book is for you. You'll meet Lucy, Sophia, Maya, Erin, and Leila—five Girls Who Code who will tell you all about coding! There are some of our favorite activities from our programs in this journal, like creating a collage that represents a topic you love, or playing a game with a friend to learn how to think like a computer. Girls across the country—and the world—use these activities to help inspire them to make amazing things through coding!

If you enjoy the activities in this book, I hope you'll come to one of our free coding clubs. We're building a sisterhood of tens of thousands of girls who use coding to be creative—and we'd love for you to join us.

Happy reading—and coding!

Reshma Saujani

Meet the Girls Who Code

Lucy

Birthday: May 20
Likes: science, music, gardening, emojis, trying new things

Sophia

Birthday: November 13
Likes: sports, sweatpants, babysitting, nail art, taking selfies

Maya

Birthday: June 3
Likes: writing, drawing, fashion, chunky jewelry, giving advice

Erin

Birthday: February 26
Likes: baking, theater, reading, surfing, doing silly impressions

Leila

Birthday: August 22
Likes: robotics, video games, field hockey, crafting, hanging out with her big sister

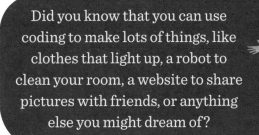

Did you know that you can use coding to make lots of things, like clothes that light up, a robot to clean your room, a website to share pictures with friends, or anything else you might dream of?

Before we start creating things with code, let's talk about what coding is. It technically means writing commands in a programming language to tell a computer what to do.

Sound boring? It's not! It's actually really fun! And coding isn't just for people who like math and science; it's for anyone who likes to be creative and to work on projects with friends.

Actually, coding is just one part of computer science, which is the study of computers—how they work and how they're designed. Coding is for anyone who wants to imagine something and use a computer to create it!

And that's exactly what this book is for! Coming up with ideas for coding can be tough, especially when there are so many possibilities. This book is a place for you to be creative and get inspired—you can doodle, draw, be silly, be serious, and even play games with your friends. You can keep track of all your ideas for coding projects here, share them with your friends, and then make them a reality!

Dream It Up

You already know that coding is writing commands in a programming language that a computer can understand—and that it's just one part of computer science. But it's an important part, because it's how you get a computer to do all the cool things you dream up.

One of the hardest—but most fun!—things about coding is figuring out what you want to make with code. For example, do you want to create a game, build a website, or make a robot dance? It can be helpful to think about what you're passionate about. Are you interested in animals, space, the environment, or maybe helping out your friends?

This section is a place for you to come up with ideas, write about them or draw them, and keep track of what inspires you. So put your creative thinking cap on, and start dreaming!

CHOOSE YOUR OWN ADVENTURE

If you could go on a journey, like a "choose your own adventure," anywhere in the world or in your imagination, where would you go, and what would it look like? Would you take anyone with you? Maybe your best friends, your family, or your pets? How would you travel? By spaceship? Submarine? What obstacles might you have to overcome? Evil elves? Space creatures? Is there a goal you'd want to reach at the end of your journey? Maybe to get somewhere new, or to have a new skill or magic power? Write and/or draw your adventure here.

. . . .

. . . .

. . . .

. . . .

. . . .

. . . .

. . . .

. . . .

. . . .

. . . .

Adventures in Coding

That was a fun fantastical trip into your imagination! Now that your brain is warmed up, try taking the same ideas and think about how you could apply them to a coding project. If you're interested in fashion, you could make clothing that adjusts to people's temperatures. If you like animals, you could make an app to help dogs at shelters get adopted. Think about what it is you want to make—a game, an app, or maybe a robot—and write or draw your ideas here.

There's no such thing as a bad idea. The point is to get as many thoughts out as you can, no matter how silly or unrealistic they may seem.

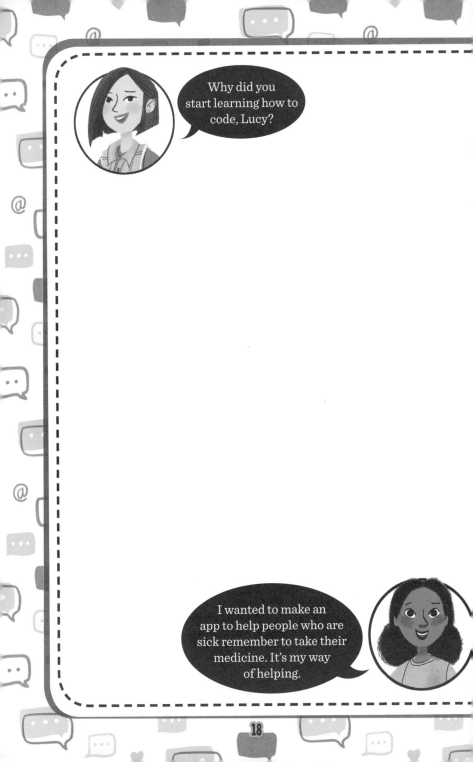

What's Coding, Anyway?

You've already learned that coding is, very simply, a way to communicate with your computer. But computers don't understand instructions the same way that people do. You have to give computers information, or *data*, in a very specific way.

Here are a few key words that will help you understand a little bit about how to organize information when you start to code. Find them in the word search, and turn the page to learn what they mean!

Word Bank

- input
- programming
- language
- variables

- loop
- conditional
- algorithm
- function

- string
- debug
- boolean
- binary code

```
S G P O T T D R F Y E T A U V S P C Y N
X G R E U V B U W Z G L G J F E H M J T
W H S P M H N G J K A N E A D F O R Z K
X B N W E C O M R N U S N F U N U R B A
Q I S G T P P U O Y G B Y S Q U I A M F
V Q Q I C H Y I P Q N P Q I O V G T P A
C O O O D L T Q H J A V O L F Q H C A L
H N P R B I D N Y Q L O V F G N A B Z G
W E T I D R O Q A Z G N A E L O O B X O
C G K N L I G S Y W N V S Z T K M O U R
F N O Y Z U T T I O I C G F Z X R G V I
V C F H K D F V J U M T V N W A D U W T
O A Z N X S U O W A M L W F I L I B I H
X F R O G T K A T Q A O J V M R J E H M
A X C I G Z B I N A R Y C O D E T D S U
D V D Y A K W R N L G U Z V E T Z S G T
A L O O P B P N T Q O D Z M N L J N S A
N R U N V T L W K C R I I Z W W G M Q Z
Z Q P D S H M E E P P K S Z E H U A N X
X S K U Z O A W S O V I P K J S P B Q O
```

Input: Input is any information that you put into a computer to get it to perform a task or make a calculation.

Programming language: A programming language is a set of rules and instructions used to write computer programs. There are many different programming languages that you can use to do different things.

Variables: Variables are like containers that are used in a program to store and remember information. Variables can hold numbers, strings of letters, and even whether something is true or false!

> So many new words! It feels like a lot to learn.

Loop: Loops are a way of writing one piece of code that repeats multiple times. If you want to draw a square, you can write one loop that says "go straight, then turn right" and have that repeat four times instead of writing it all out.

Conditional: Conditionals are elements of code that happen only if something else happens. Conditionals are also called *if statements*, because *if* something is true, then another thing will happen.

Algorithm: An algorithm is a set of steps that a computer follows to complete a task. You can write algorithms that do all kinds of things, from solving math problems to writing music!

Function: A function is a list of steps in a program that are all wrapped up together. When you give information, or *input*, to the function, it processes that information and gives you back an answer, or an *output*.

String: A string is a data type made up of characters that can include letters, spaces, and numbers. You can usually tell something is a string if it's in quotation marks—even numbers can be strings! Some examples of strings are "girlswhocode" and "girls who code" and "12345."

Debug: A process for figuring out why your code is not working as you planned, and fixing the problems.

I know, but I bet that with a little time, we'll be able to "decode" some of coding's key ideas. See what I did there? Ha!

Boolean: In coding, booleans are a data type made up of true or false options that help your computer know what to do as it works through your code. Booleans are used in *if statements*, where if the statement is true, then something will happen, but if the statement is false, then something different will happen.

Binary code: Binary code represents words or computer processor instructions into a series of 1s and 0s that tell computers what to do. In binary code, the word *hi* is 01101000 01101001.

YEP, YOU CAN MAKE THAT WITH CODE!

So, what are you going to make with code? There are tons of cool (and some surprising!) things made with code. Circle the items that you think have been made (or enhanced) with code, and check your answers in the back of the book.

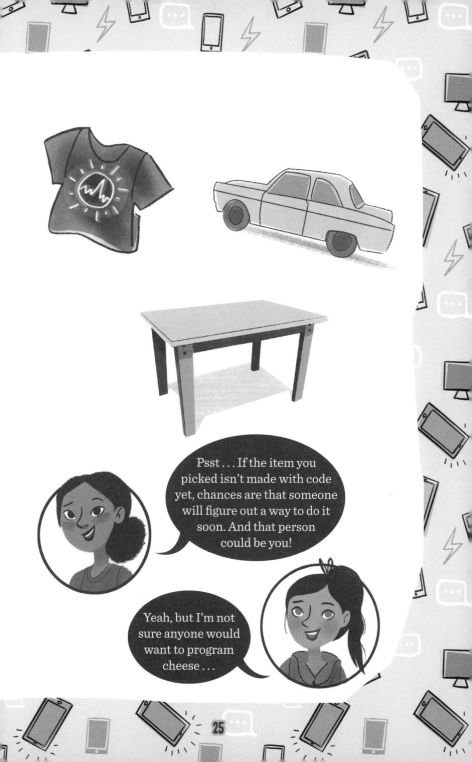

Psst... If the item you picked isn't made with code yet, chances are that someone will figure out a way to do it soon. And that person could be you!

Yeah, but I'm not sure anyone would want to program cheese...

What Are You Going to Make?

Getting started on a new idea or project can be tough, no matter what it is. That's why it can be helpful to brainstorm (come up with ideas) by yourself or with friends. Any ideas, no matter how far-fetched they seem, are fair game! The point is to think freely and see what you can come up with.

What is something you always wish you had? Maybe it's something just for fun, like a game or toy? Or maybe it's a tool?

_____

_____

_____

_____

_____

_____

Is there a device or an app that could help keep you organized, help you remember things, or help you stay in touch with your friends and family?

_____

_____

_____

_____

_____

_____

_____

_____

_____

_____

_____

_____

_____

Is there something your friends, family, or teachers say they wish they had? How would it work?

_____

_____

_____

_____

_____

_____

_____

If you could invent any machine, what would it be? What would it do? Who else might like it? Why?

_____

_____

_____

_____

_____

_____

_____

What's something you use all the time that could work better (like a watch, water bottle, etc.)? How could you improve it or make it just right for you?

_____

_____

_____

_____

_____

_____

_____

Collage This!

What topics, jobs, and causes are you interested in? The environment? Fashion? Animals? Sports? Cooking? Music? Make a collage that represents what you're passionate about. You can use images from magazines and articles, and add quotes, logos, flags, and photos, or anything else you'd like. You can write and draw on your collage, too!

I'm going to put my favorite quote from Peter Pan in my collage: "The moment you doubt whether you can fly, you cease forever to be able to do it."

Ooh—I like that quote. I'm going to put photos from my favorite sports teams on mine.

Inspiration Central

When you're having trouble finding inspiration, try asking yourself questions to get your creative juices flowing. This could even help you come up with an idea for what to code!

Do you have a role model who inspires you? Who is it, and why do they inspire you?

_____

_____

_____

_____

Is there a cause you care about deeply? What is it, and why is it important to you?

_____

_____

_____

_____

_____

_____

What's your favorite
hobby? What do you
love about it?

_____

_____

_____

_____

_____

_____

_____

Design This!

When creating a program or an app, it can be helpful to have a visual of what you want it to look like. Use these pages to think of design elements that inspire you. What are your favorite colors? Are there certain colors that make you happy or sad? What about fonts? Do you like to handwrite things yourself?

Write, draw, and use images from magazines, stamps, stickers, or logos from food boxes to show what kind of designs you like.

I love coming up with different handwriting, like these really fancy letters.

That looks awesome. My handwriting is awful, but I can type really fast!

Mood Boards

Create a mood board that represents sadness to you. What are the colors or images that you think of when you're feeling blue?

Now create a mood board that represents happiness to you. Use colors, images, and words that make you smile!

Let's Think About It!

Once you have an idea for something to make with code, it's important to do a little research *and* a little bit of deep thinking about what you plan to make. Is it doable, will it be useful to other people, and are you sure you want to spend your time making it?

Here's a handy flowchart to help you answer some of these questions.

Do We Need It?

Not Sure

Yes

Ask your friends and family for input.

Congrats! A good idea! Go to next question.

Does It Already Exist?

Yes

No

Can we make it better? Keep researching.

Congrats! A new useful product! Go to next question.

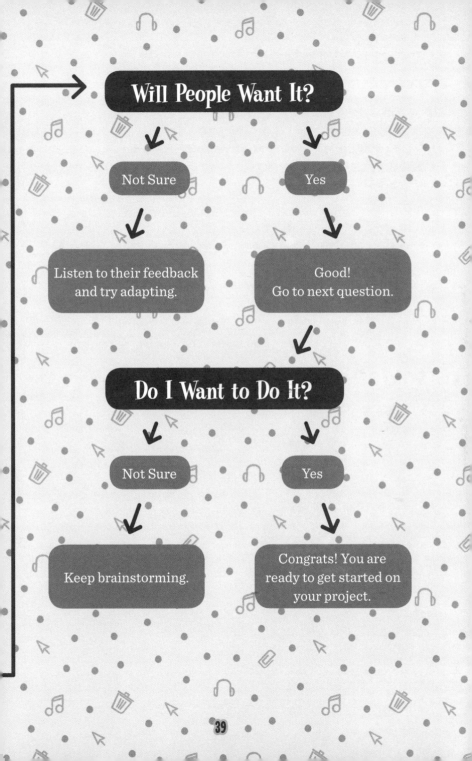

Will People Want It?

Not Sure

Yes

Listen to their feedback and try adapting.

Good!
Go to next question.

Do I Want to Do It?

Not Sure

Yes

Keep brainstorming.

Congrats! You are ready to get started on your project.

Extra, Extra, Read All About It!

A great technique for thinking through your idea is to imagine it finished. If you could write a front-page headline in *The Coding Times* announcing your new creation and the impact it's having, what would your headline be? Make it bold and fun! Talk about how people are using your invention, or how it's changing the world. What does it do? What are its cool, amazing, newsworthy features?

I'm making a robot that helps blind people by letting them know when there's something in front of them.

That sounds awesome!

The Coding Times

The Coding Times

Top Secret!

Secret codes and ciphers (a type of code that replaces individual letters with other letters, numbers, or symbols) have been used to hide important messages for thousands of years. This practice is called cryptography, and computers are great at it. In fact, some of the earliest computing machines were built in the 1940s to both encrypt and crack codes during World War II!

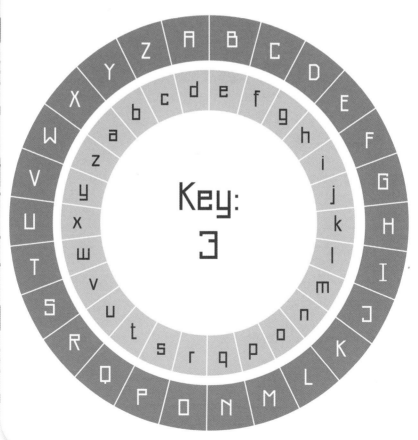

Key:
3

This is a Caesar cipher, which was used by the famous Roman emperor Julius Caesar. It's a simple way to hide a message.

Exactly. By turning the wheel, you shift the letters of the alphabet down by as many steps as you choose. That lets you turn an *A* into a *C*, for instance. That way, you can scramble your message so that it's harder to read!

See if you can decode the following message:

frglqj lv dzhvrph !

_ _ _ _ _ _   _ _   _ _ _ _ _ _ _

Here's your own Caesar cipher.

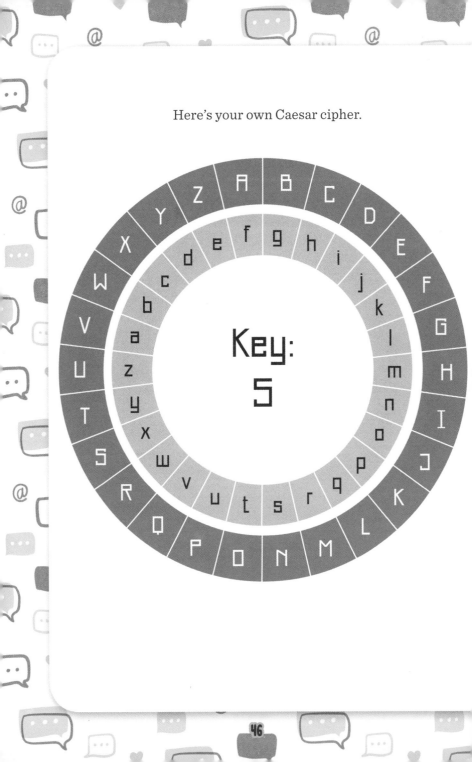

Key:
5

Now try encrypting your own message using the wheel.
Write one here, put it into code, and have a friend decode it!

Message:

_____

_____

_____

_____

_____

Code:

_____

_____

_____

_____

_____

Let's Get Started!

Now that you've learned some basic coding terminology, brainstormed ideas, and thought about what kind of designs you like, are you ready to dive into coding? There are lots of ways to begin. Often getting started on a big project is the hardest part. This section is full of tips and tricks to help get the ball rolling—or the keys clicking!

CAN'T STOP THE FEELING

How do you feel when you start a new project or task? Overwhelmed, excited, inspired, or maybe scared? Write or draw how you feel at the beginning of a challenge, like studying for a test, planning a party, or any other big project.

For me, it depends on the project. If it's a dress design or collage, I can't wait to get started. But if it's cleaning my room, that's a whole other story.

When I have to clean my room, I start with one easy thing, like picking up my clothes or making my bed. Before I know it, I'm halfway done and it's easy to finish the rest!

What are the easiest and hardest parts of projects for you? Write down how you feel about each stage: Excited? Nervous? Overwhelmed? Right on track? Over it? Into it? You can think of a specific project or lots of different ones!

PLANNING

_____

_____

_____

_____

_____

_____

_____

STARTING

_____

_____

_____

_____

_____

_____

_____

DOING THE WORK

_____
_____
_____
_____
_____
_____

FINISHING THE PROJECT

_____
_____
_____
_____

SHARING THE PROJECT

_____
_____
_____
_____
_____

Emoj-ician!

Sometimes when you're nervous 😓 or overwhelmed 😖, it helps to think about a time you felt confident 😎, happy 😊, or determined 😤, to remind you that you've got what it takes to tackle anything you set your mind to.

As you answer the questions below, draw in the emoji that best describes your feeling.

1. Describe a time you solved a problem and got a good result. How did it make you feel to know you could do it?

_____

_____

_____

_____

_____

_____

_____

2. Was there a time you tried something new that you weren't sure about, and realized you really liked it? How do you feel about that thing now?

_____

_____

_____

_____

_____

_____

_____

3. Describe a time something didn't go your way, but you didn't give up. What was it that gave you the strength to keep pushing?

_____

_____

_____

_____

_____

_____

_____

Girl Power: Famous Women in Coding History

There are many amazing women who have contributed to computer science throughout the years. Here are just a few!

Ada Lovelace

Augusta "Ada" Byron Lovelace is considered the world's first programmer. In 1843, at the age of twenty-seven, she published a set of notes about an early example of a proposed mechanical computer. Her notes included step-by-step operating instructions for how to program it. Although computers didn't exist at the time, this turned out to be the world's first computer program. Today a programming language used to control space satellites is called Ada in her honor.

Are you surprised to find out the first computer programmer was a woman? Why or why not? Do you know (or have you heard of) any other women programmers? Who are they, and how do they inspire you?

Grace Murray Hopper

Modern coding wouldn't exist if it weren't for Grace Hopper (1906–1992). A mathematician and rear admiral in the US Navy, Grace invented the compiler, a system that takes human readable programming language and translates it into binary code. She also helped popularize the term *debugging* in computing after the team she was working with traced the cause of a malfunction in their computer to a moth that had gotten in the hardware. To fix it, they had to debug the computer (literally!). That's why we debug when we work out a problem in our code!

Have you ever popularized a term for something? What was it? If you could invent new words to describe how you feel about something or how you would go about creating a project, what would they be?

Katherine Johnson

Katherine Johnson was born in West Virginia in 1918. As an African American woman, she broke race and gender barriers when she joined NACA, the National Advisory Committee for Aeronautics, as a mathematician. A few years later, NACA became NASA, the National Aeronautics and Space Administration. A math genius and "human computer," Katherine made precise calculations that planned the trajectory to safely send the first American into orbit and land the first humans on the moon. In the 1960s, computers were still a new technology. Katherine's work double-checking the calculations that computers were producing helped convince NASA of the value of this new technology.

Did you know the first computers in space had less computing power than a pocket calculator? How do you think computers will change in the coming years? Will they get smaller, bigger, or become different kinds of machines entirely?

Better Together

Coding isn't something you have to do alone at a computer—it's something you can do with your friends! In fact, most of the time, projects get better and problems get solved faster when you work as a team.

So find a friend and try this algorithm game!

You know that algorithms are precise step-by-step instructions on how to do something. The goal of this game is to give a friend clear instructions on how to perform a task while blindfolded. Think you can do it? Let's try!

What You'll Need

- Blindfold
- Three books
- At least one friend

Find a spot in a room with a table. Spread the books on the table in three different places. Take a couple of steps back and blindfold your friend. Give your friend a spin around, and then, using step-by-step directions, tell them how to walk to the table, pick up a book, and stack it on top of another book, until all three are stacked.

How'd you do? Were there some instructions that worked better than others? What would you do differently if you played this game again?

MY BESTIES AND ME

Coding is much more fun when you work on projects with friends. Everyone brings something different to the table, which makes the end result so much better. Use these pages to write about you and your besties.

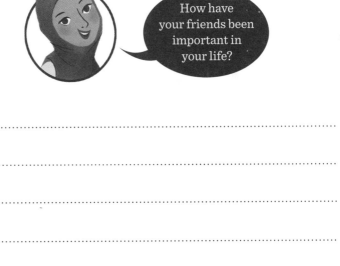

How have your friends been important in your life?

....
....
....
....
....
....
....
....

Do you have a friend who always makes you laugh?

....

....

....

....

Do you have a friend who always listens to your problems?

....

....

....

....

....

....

Who are some friends you can always count on?

....

....

....

....

How are your friends helping you learn about coding? What are you learning from one another?

....

....

....

....

....

....

....

Do your friends give you advice? Good ideas? Like what? How can you be an even better friend to your besties?

....

....

....

....

....

....

....

....

....

....

....

....

PLAN AWAY!

Big projects need to be broken into little steps, kind of as if you're climbing a mountain. You can't just charge straight up, or you might get tired really quickly—or worse, get lost. But if you find a foothold and move carefully, knowing your plan and your goal (to reach the top, right?), you'll make it!

Marathon Maze

Use the same ideas from the mountain maze here. Thinking about tackling an entire marathon might be intimidating, but if you approach it one step at a time, it'll feel more manageable—just like a coding project!

START

Remember to pace yourself!

FINISH

Best App in the World

User experience (or UX) is an area of design that looks at how people interact with digital products and devices. Think about how your phone automatically rotates a video to be wide-screen if you turn it sideways. Have you ever wondered how a phone knows to do that? It's because a designer thought about the best way to watch a video on a phone, and worked with a programmer who coded it that way. Pretty cool, huh?

Now it's *your* turn to be a UX designer! Imagine you've invented a mobile app that reminds you when it's someone's birthday and automatically sends a "HAPPY BIRTHDAY" text to that person from your phone. Draw your design of the app here.

Your app got reviewed! Color in the stars. How many did you get?

Now write the review. Imagine what consumers are saying. What words do they use to describe your invention? What makes it so special, great, successful, difficult to use, or different?

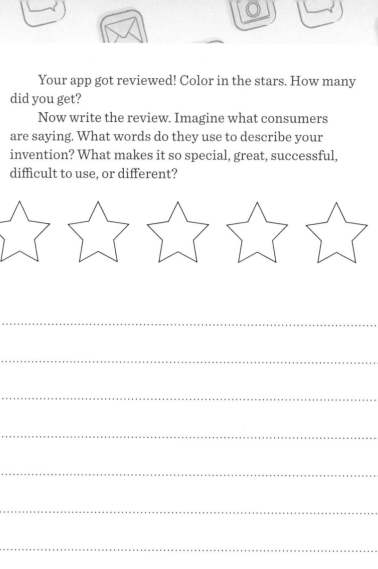

Best App in the World

Draw people using your app. What's their reaction? What do they like about it? Could it be better? What's not working? Why? How can this kind of feedback help you design a better experience?

Make-Believe

Game design is a way to map out a game so programmers get an idea of where it's going and what they need to build. Try making your own characters, world, and destination! Here are three templates. Fill them in with details for a game you'd like to make.

My favorite games are about superhero girls who save the day!

Those are fun! I especially like games about friendship.

Draw the hero of your game

Are you a wizard, a space pirate, an oceanographer, or something else?

Draw the world they are moving through

Is it a fantasy forest, an asteroid field, an ocean, or something else?

Draw their destination

Is it a castle, an alien planet, a deep-sea crevasse, or something else?

Frame of Mind

Wireframes are a way of organizing visual information to help designers and programmers plan out what's in an app or website. You know how when you write a story, you sometimes write an outline first? Well, a wireframe is kind of like a visual outline—a sketch of what's going to be created.

Here's an example of a wireframe for a mobile app:

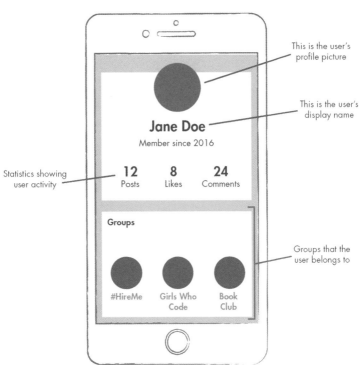

This is the user's profile picture

This is the user's display name

Jane Doe
Member since 2016

Statistics showing user activity

12	**8**	**24**
Posts	Likes	Comments

Groups

#HireMe   Girls Who Code   Book Club

Groups that the user belongs to

Now try drawing your own wireframe for something you want to create with code. What features do you want to include? Label what each feature does.

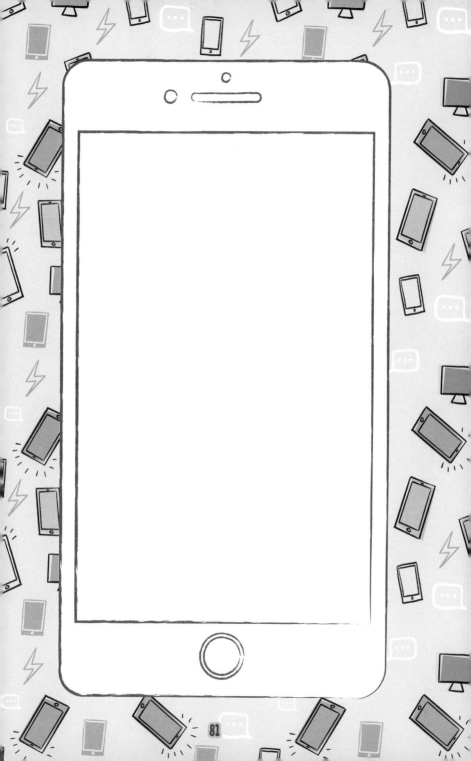

Do You Speak Code?

A programming language is the type of code that you input into your computer to give it commands in a language it can understand. Easy-peasy, right? But there are actually hundreds of different programming languages that are used to communicate code to computers, and each language has programming jobs that it's specialized for.

Here are a few descriptions of different languages and what they're often used for. See if you can find them on the next page!

Python is a programming language great for getting started, and you can use it to do all sorts of things. Python can be used to create web applications, and it's a great language for beginners, because learning Python first helps you learn other languages later.

Scratch was developed by the MIT Media Lab to teach people of all ages to code using drag-and-drop blocks that help you learn basic coding commands without worrying about forgetting something. Scratch lets you design and code interactive stories that you can then share with the community.

Javascript is a language that was created to help artists learn to code by giving instant visual feedback, and uses a simplified version of Java as its foundation.

Java is a programming language that is often used to create Android apps. Java works for all platforms and devices, and because it's stable and has been around for a long time, people love it for big projects. Java is everywhere!

HTML, or "Hypertext Markup Language," is the language that people use most to create webpages. HTML defines the structure of a webpage, which can then be styled using CSS.

CSS, or "Cascading Style Sheets," is a language used to describe how the HTML elements on a webpage look. One CSS file can control the style and layout of multiple webpages! CSS and HTML are BFFs, and you won't often see one without the other. Although you'll still need a programming language to do things like loops and conditionals, these markup languages are very important for laying out and designing your page.

Swift is a programming language used for making iPhone and iPad apps.

Ruby is a general purpose programming language similar to Python, often used for making web applications.

Binary is a series of 1s and 0s, converted from other programming languages, that tell computers what to do. For example, in binary code, the word "hi" is 01101000 01101001.

Find the programming languages in this word search.

But watch out for Python—I hear it bites! Ha!

Word Bank

- Python
- Scratch
- Javascript
- Java
- HTML
- CSS
- Ruby
- Swift
- Binary

```
B  A  J  N  S  K  T  D  U  J  V  D  X  N  B
I  H  B  S  M  C  S  F  G  Z  U  M  G  U  Y
N  G  F  G  N  L  R  L  M  T  H  L  F  E  B
A  W  L  S  Z  Z  D  A  Y  V  K  J  B  B  U
R  N  Z  U  N  G  X  P  T  B  Q  E  C  D  R
Y  P  U  D  C  I  V  L  X  C  U  X  W  W  N
F  S  I  J  X  S  I  N  J  H  H  B  K  A  T
T  E  S  J  G  S  W  D  W  M  E  U  J  A  P
Q  X  A  C  U  Y  S  I  U  I  D  P  Q  V  I
W  V  J  D  B  V  K  W  F  D  Y  Y  V  F  Y
A  Q  T  T  Y  C  I  H  Q  T  K  T  X  Q  B
J  A  V  A  S  C  R  I  P  T  M  H  G  G  U
E  S  G  U  R  G  Z  T  H  C  R  U  E  N  A
E  K  H  R  L  A  H  H  Z  M  T  N  L  Z  C
K  K  W  G  U  I  H  Y  U  W  B  P  L  J  L
```

Troubleshooting

Nothing you do goes right 100 percent of the time, right? Maybe your model rocket failed to launch, you put your hair in a fancy up-do that totally frizzed out, or your grandma's famous muffin recipe ended in mush. Sometimes things just don't work the way you planned, especially when you're creating something new. That's where troubleshooting, or tracking down and trying to solve problems, can be a big help. This section is all about coming up with ideas for how to do just that!

Feature Creep

Feature creep is when you keep adding new ideas, or features, that you might not need to a project. Those features "creep" in, making your project more complicated than it needs to be.

Now draw your own robot! Pick one thing that you want the robot to be good at (like playing chess, baking, or folding clothes, for example) and design it—but without adding too many features. What's the robot's key feature and what does it do?

Key feature: _____

What does it do: _____

# Rubber Duck It

One way programmers like to problem solve is by describing the problem to a rubber duck on their desk. Seems silly, right? But it often works, because talking through a problem out loud can help you figure it out. For example, have you ever told a friend or family member about a problem, but figured out the solution while you were explaining it to them?

Write out a problem or obstacle you're facing, whether it's with coding or something else in your life. Maybe you're having a fight with a friend, or your team lost a soccer game. See if writing it out helps you solve it.

Describe the problem:

_____

_____

_____

_____

_____

_____

_____

_____

_____

Where are you stuck?

_____

_____

_____

_____

_____

_____

_____

_____

_____

_____

_____

_____

_____

_____

_____

_____

_____

_____

What have you tried?

_____

_____

_____

_____

_____

_____

_____

_____

What could you try that's different?

_____

_____

_____

_____

_____

_____

_____

_____

_____

_____

_____

_____

_____

Who can help you?

_____

_____

_____

_____

_____

_____

_____

_____

WORDS OF WISDOM

Sometimes when I feel down, I look through my book of quotes for inspiration. Here are some of my favorites!

"We must have perseverance, and above all confidence in ourselves. We must believe that we are gifted for something, and that this thing, at whatever cost, must be attained."

—Marie Curie, scientist, first woman to win a Nobel Prize

"I don't work at something because I think it's important. I work at things that, to me, are interesting."

—Eugenie Clark, scientist and shark expert, also known as the Shark Lady

"Work with others. It helps when you have self-doubts, because you're in it together. You share the successes together, and the failures aren't as much of a failure."

–Ayanna Howard, American roboticist

"The most damaging phrase in the English language is 'we've always done it this way!'"

–Grace Hopper, computer scientist, inventor of the compiler

"It often takes many, many tries until that magical moment when what you're trying to build comes to life. It requires perseverance. It requires imperfection. Be brave, not perfect."

–Reshma Saujani, founder of Girls Who Code

These are awesome, Erin! I feel pumped to get back to my projects!

Inspire Yourself

Is there a saying or quote that inspires you? Or maybe an image that always makes you feel proud or strong? Write it down or sketch it out here. Bookmark the page so you can easily find it the next time you need a dose of encouragement.

Spot the Error in the Error Message

You can get error messages when you're coding—and that's okay! An error message is your computer's way of letting you know that you've made a mistake in some part of your code. It can be as simple as a misspelled word or missing piece of punctuation, or it can indicate a bigger problem with how you're designing your program. Whatever the message is, think of it as an opportunity to learn something and fix what's wrong!

This game will give you a chance to get familiar with error messages, what they look like, and what they mean. Look at the code on the grid below. That's the CORRECT code to get the duck through the maze successfully.

```
duck.swimDown(2);
duck.turnLeft( );
duck.swimForward(2);
```

Finish!

Now take a look at the code below. One of the lines has a small error in it. Can you spot it? Match the error to the explanation of what's wrong with your code.

Wrong object

```
duck.swimDown(2)
duck.turnLeft( );
duck.swimForward(2);
```

Missing semicolon

```
duck.swimDown(2);
duck.turnRight( );
duck.swimForward(2);
```

Wrong distance

```
car.moveDown(2);
car.turnLeft( );
car.moveForward(2);
```

Wrong turn directions

```
duck.swimDown(1);
duck.turnLeft( );
duck.swimForward(1);
```

Oooh, I hate error messages.

Yeah, they're no fun, but I like figuring out how to fix them!

Debugging Log

When a situation isn't working the way you think it should (maybe a homework assignment, a dance routine, or a song you're trying to write), sometimes it helps to do a little detective work to figure out what went wrong. Try looking at the problem from a fresh angle, think about what you've tried, consider what's working or not working, and see if you can solve the problem.

In coding, this process is called debugging. When you do it for coding, it's a great idea to keep track of what's working and what's not working in your code. Here's a handy log to help you, no matter what the problem.

Date: _____

Project name: _____

What's not working? _____

_____

How have you tried to solve the problem? What steps did you try?

❏ Retracing your steps

❏ Talking about the problem with a friend

❏ Taking a break and checking in later

❏ Other: _____

Did it work? _____

_____

_____

_____

_____

_____

_____

_____

_____

_____

Date: _____

Project name: _____

What's not working? _____

_____

How have you tried to solve the problem? What steps did you try?

❑ Retracing your steps
❑ Talking about the problem with a friend
❑ Taking a break and checking in later
❑ Other: _____

Did it work? _____

_____

_____

_____

_____

_____

_____

_____

_____

_____

Date: _____

Project name: _____

What's not working? _____

_____

How have you tried to solve the problem? What steps did you try?

- ❏ Retracing your steps
- ❏ Talking about the problem with a friend
- ❏ Taking a break and checking in later
- ❏ Other: _____

Did it work? _____

_____

_____

_____

_____

_____

_____

_____

_____

_____

_____

We've Got the Tools!

Learning to code is just like learning how to cook, paint, sew, or play an instrument. You have to learn the basic rules, and then let your creativity take over! The rules are just tools to help you create anything you can imagine. With these tools, if you can dream it, you can do it!

LET'S TALK ABOUT IT

You're doing it! If you've gotten to this part, you've already accomplished so much. You can keep learning, growing, and getting better and better at coding—or whatever you choose to do. Write a bit about what you've learned so far.

WHAT'S BEEN YOUR FAVORITE PART OF LEARNING ABOUT CODING?

_____

_____

_____

_____

WHAT HAVE YOU LEARNED ABOUT DEALING WITH PROBLEMS IN CODING?

_____

_____

WHAT'S YOUR BIGGEST DREAM ABOUT WHAT YOU COULD DO WITH CODING?

DO YOU FEEL LIKE YOU COULD DO IT?

WHAT DO YOU STILL WANT TO LEARN ABOUT CODING?

Supersecret Tips, Tricks, and Hacks

If you've been coding and sharing ideas with your friends, chances are you've come up with lots of ways to solve problems and work together.

Here's a spot to write down what you've learned—your best hacks, tips, tricks, and ideas.

_____

_____

_____

_____

_____

_____

_____

_____

_____

_____

_____

_____

_____

Answer Key

p. 20–21; What's Coding, Anyway?

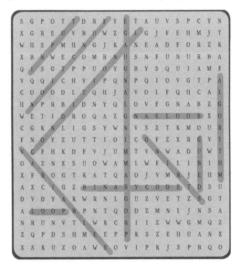

p. 24–25; Yep, You Can Make That with Code

Cars: Code is used to make all the software inside cars work smoothly and safely, and now, many computer scientists are working on code that allows cars to safely drive themselves!

Clothing: Want to be super fashionable? Program your own clothing by sewing sensors into the fabric! You can make it light up or regulate to your body temperature.

Phones and tablets: Millions of lines of code written by thousands of different computer scientists allow phones and tablets to do everything from playing games and creating art to taking pictures and, yes, even making phone calls.

p. 44–45; Top Secret!

Answer: Coding is awesome!

Missing semicolon
```
duck.swimDown(2)
duck.turnLeft();
duck.swimForward(2);
```
Wrong turn directions
```
duck.swimDown(2);
duck.turnRight();
duck.swimForward(2);
```
Wrong object
```
car.moveDown(2);
car.turnLeft();
car.moveForward(2);
```
Wrong distance
```
duck.swimDown(1);
duck.turnLeft();
duck.swimForward(1);
```

To learn more about how to code, don't miss: